You'll also need a mound of sand (you can find that at the beach), a shovel, and a bucket to carry water and sand.

Wall tool/scraper

Rake/shovel

Let's get started! Dig Your Sand Quarry

Claim a piece of land to build your kingdom. Workers would use oxen to pull carts filled with stone to the site. Choose a spot close enough to the waterline so your oxen won't have to travel far. You must have water mixed in with the sand to build a strong fortress – dry sand will crumble.

There are two ways to get the perfect sand for your castle . . .

1. At the beach, if you dig a deep hole (get an adult assistant to help) in the sand close to the tideline, you will soon hit water! This hole will now be your sand quarry – this sand is the perfect wetness for building your castle.

2.

You can also turn your bucket into a sand quarry. Fill your bucket with water and scoop sand into the bucket – let the water drain and flow over the sides.

It's easy to build a tower!

Towers were tall so castle guards could see for miles around. When soldiers attacked a castle, they used a battering ram to knock down a tower. Round towers were stronger than square towers because there were no corners for the battering ram to hit.

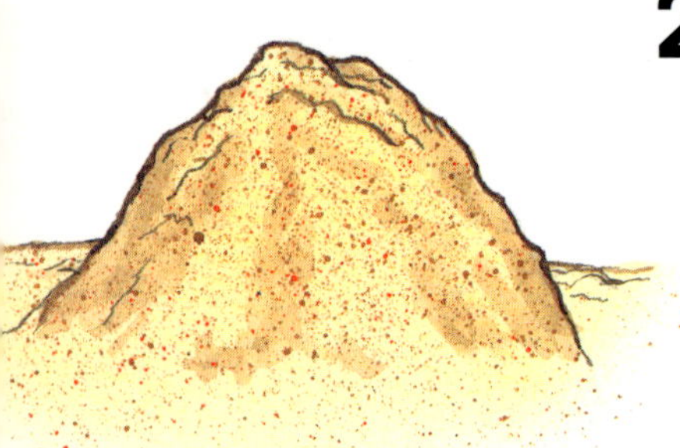

2. Take the round turret cap and place it on the bottom of the turret ring. The four bumps of the ring should fit into the holes on the cap.

1. Scoop sand from your sand quarry and pile it on top of itself. Continue to do this until you get the height you want (start small at first . . .).

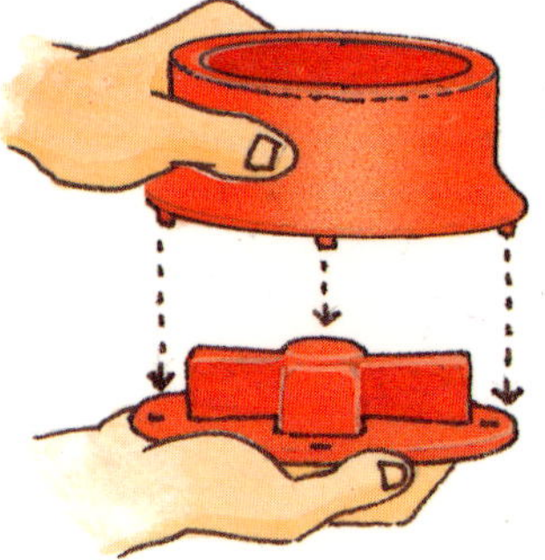

3. Scoop and pat wet sand into the mold. Use the wall tool/scraper to smooth the sand at the top of the filled mold.

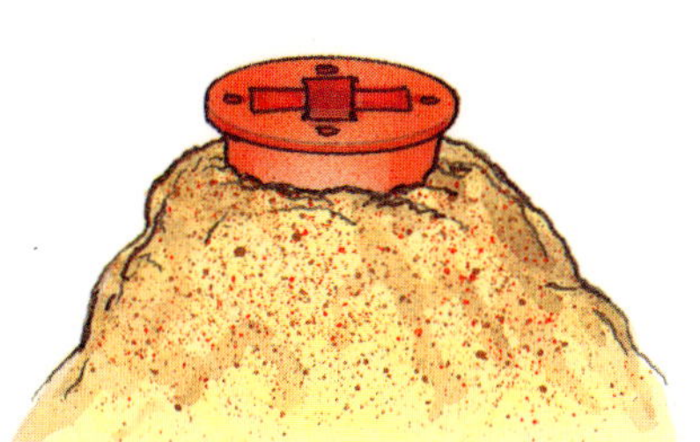

4. Flip the mold over on top of your sand mound.

5. Lift the cap straight off the turret ring.

6. Slide the ring down. As you pull the ring down, wipe off excess sand that accumulates around it.

7. *Slowly* and *carefully* pull the ring up and off the tower. With a little practice, you will be a master tower builder!

Up go the castle walls!

A wall was built around the castle to protect the king and his kingdom during attacks. The walls around the castle had crenels (the slots at the top) through which the soldiers could defend the castle.

1. Mound up wet sand between your towers. Pat the mound to make it strong.

It is best to build your towers first, then connect them with walls.

3. Take the outside of the wall tool/scraper and shave the inner side of the wall clean. Also use the wall tool/scraper to clean up left over sand around your towers. Now your guards can keep watch over your castle!

2. Take the wall tool/scraper and push it down to mold crenels on the outer side of the wall.

Level 1 The Norman Castle

Build a square tower surrounded by a wall with four round guard towers and raked grounds.

Always build the inside of the castle first and then the outside walls.

1. Build the center square tower.
2. Build the four round outer towers. To decide the distance between towers, use the wall tool/scraper to measure out exactly one, two, or three lengths of the wall tool/scraper between towers. That way you can be sure that your wall tool/scraper will fit nicely between towers.
3. Now build walls to connect your towers.
4. Use your rake to clean the grounds inside the walls. After all, it must be fit for a king or queen!

he Normans brought knights and castles to England. Some of the first castles built in England were called Norman Keeps. They were single towers with one entrance high above the ground to keep unwanted intruders out.

Level 2 Gandolf Castle

Build a castle made of square and round towers on top of a hill. Surround it by a wall with five guard towers, a main entrance, and a moat.

Always build the inside of the castle first and then the outside walls.

1. Many castles were built on a natural hill for safety. Pile and continually pack wet sand with your hands to form a large flat mound. Use the wall tool/scraper to make a flat surface on top of the hill.

2. Build your castle. If you're having trouble with the towers toppling over, try building them shorter until you master the technique.

3. Build your wall and then dig your moat around your wall. Dig your moat far enough away from your wall to prevent any cave-ins.

4. Then dig your main entrance through the surrounding wall.

y the eleventh century, towers and walls were being built higher. Castles became larger so family, friends, knights, guards, noblemen, and workers could all live together.

A castle fit for a king or queen!

Royal castles were built to glorify the king. They were carved with fancy designs. Detailing your sandcastle will take patience and a steady hand. The key is to start at the top and work your way down.

Moats. In medieval times trenches were dug around the outer wall. They were filled with water to protect the kingdom from attackers. Use your hands or the wall tool/scraper to dig your moat.

Raking. Use your rake/shovel to clean and smooth the courtyard around your castle. Remember that royalty will be walking your grounds!

Windows and Doors. Round arches called Romanesque arches were used since about the year 1100. To make windows and doors, push the shovel end of your rake/shovel tool into a wall and scrape downward, removing a thin layer of sand.

Archways. You can dig all the way through walls and towers to create an archway. Slowly scoop out sand with your hands and clean it up with the rake/shovel. Alternate between sides until you meet in the middle.

Drawbridge. The moat was crossed at the main entrance by a wood bridge called a drawbridge. To build a bridge over your moat, find some small twigs or sticks to lay across your moat.

The drawbridge was usually lifted to keep intruders out.

Stairs. Choose where you'd like your stairs to start, and use the wall tool/scraper to make a smooth slope down to where your stairs will end. Next take the rake/shovel and cut away a level platform to create a step.

Keep creating steps...

step by step!

Level 3 The Victory Castle

Adding drawbridges, roads, windows, doors and a little village.

Always build the inside of the castle first and then the outside walls.

1. Build a hill for your castle.
2. Build your castle by building square towers and round towers side by side. Add windows and doors to your castle.
3. Build a wall to protect your castle.
4. Build a village outside the castle wall. Make little huts by using the square or round tower ring without the tower cap. Use your imagination and build little huts that can serve as barns and stables.
5. Build a second wall around the village.
6. Add roads to your castle, and a moat and a drawbridge.

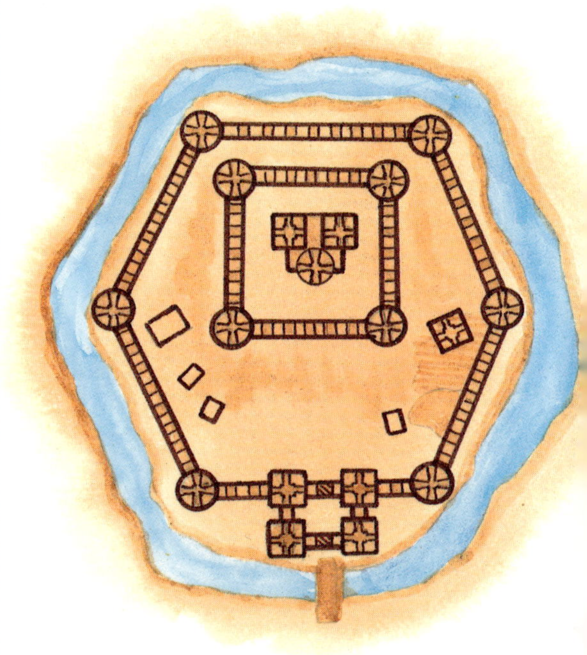

By the twelfth century, there was not only a castle within the walls, but an entire village. People built their cottages, workshops, and markets close to the castle.

Level 4 Excalibur Castle

Add stairs, archways, barbicans (towers at an entrance way) and a large village.

Always build the inside of the castle first and then the outside wall.

1. Build a large hill for your castle.
2. Build your castle on the hill first. Add all the details on your castle (windows, doors, stairs, archways) before you build the first wall around it.
3. Build your village outside the castle wall – it's your village . . . build an ice cream stand or an arcade!
4. Build a wall around your village with guard towers.
5. Build a third short wall around all of this. Dig your moat far enough away from your outside wall to prevent cave-ins. Add your barbicans.

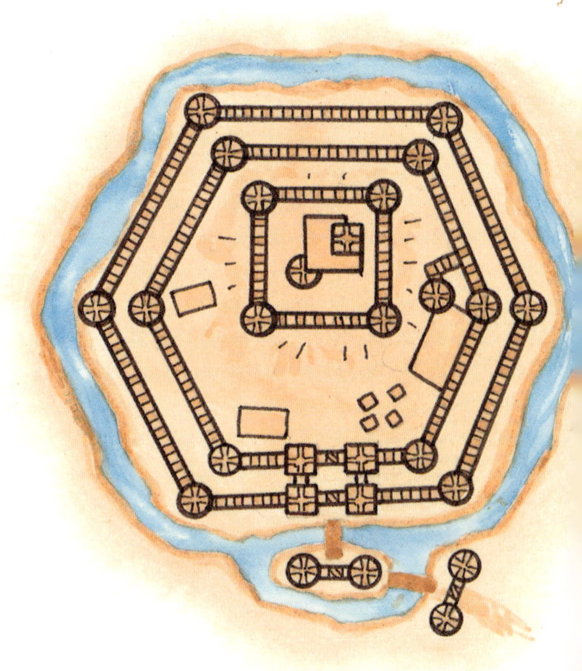

By the year 1200, castles had "concentric defenses" – the castle was protected by a moat, then a wall, then a second wall, and sometimes even a third wall. There were towers outside the wall protecting the outer entrance.

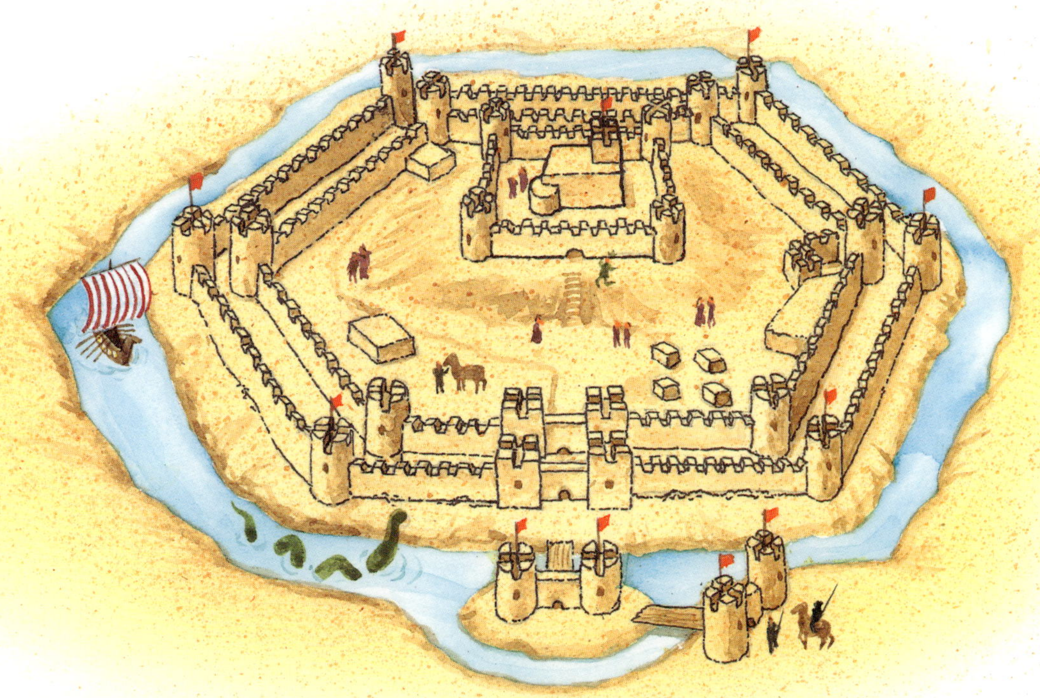

Fly your Crest over your Kingdom!

Every knight had a coat of arms, or a symbol that he passed on to his children. The royal coat of arms for each kingdom was placed on everything . . . from shields to swords to rings and trumpet banners.

Banners and flags. You can design your kingdom's coat of arms and put it on flags or banners to fly about your kingdom. In medieval times, they used moons, dragons, lions, the sun, stars . . . or just patterns of squares, diamonds, or crosses.

Take a piece of paper and cut a diamond or rectangle for your banners. Use glue or tape and fold the two halves together around a toothpick or a small stick. Decorate your flag or banner with your coat of arms!